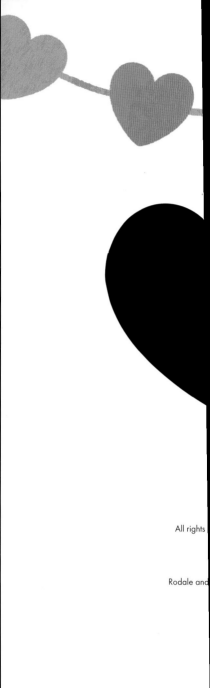

Rodale and

I LOVE YOU
EVERY DAY

BY
ISABEL OTTER

ILLUSTRATED BY
ALICIA MÁS

LOVE UNITES PEOPLE ALL OVER THE WORLD.

But what does it really mean?

Love can be a feeling or words that we say . . .

I LOVE YOU EVERY DAY.

LOVE IS AFFECTIONATE.

Great big cuddles, hugs, and kisses.

The safe nest of a warm embrace.

It can travel over borders and reach across the ocean.

LOVE MEANS TRUST.

A safe space to be ourselves.

LOVE FEELS LIKE HARMONY.

We'll snuggle up like peas in a pod.

LOVE CAN BE GENEROUS.

No matter how much we give,
it never runs out.

LOVE IS BEING CARED FOR.

Always feeling protected.

LOVE CAN MAKE US STRONG.

When we know someone believes in us,
we can do anything!

LOVE iS FAMILY.

An invisible bond that holds us all together.

LOVE IS FOUND IN FRIENDSHIP.

From play and laughter . . .

to sharing and kindness.

LOVE iS A GiFT.

It must be celebrated and looked after.

WHEN LOVE IS SHARED, IT GROWS AND GROWS!

It shines as brightly as stars.

So look for love and pass it on. . . .

LET'S SHOW LOVE EVERY DAY!

HOW DO YOU SHOW YOUR LOVE?

1.

2.

3.